For my twin sister, Julie,
for always encouraging me to do better.
— L.D.

For Henry, Mae, and Sophia at Little Tree Farms.
— D.Z.

Text copyright © 2014 Lori Degman
Illustrations copyright © 2014 Deborah Zemke
Cover and book design by Simon Stahl

Library of Congress Catalog Number 2013038643

Published by Creston Books, LLC in Berkeley, California
www.crestonbooks.co

Source of Production: Worzalla Books, Stevens Point, Wisconsin
Printed and bound in the United States of America
1 2 3 4 5

FSC
www.fsc.org
MIX
From responsible
sources
FSC® C002589

Cock-a-Doodle Oops!

by Lori Degman

illustrated by
Deborah Zemke

Farmer McPeeper was such a deep sleeper,
not even an earthquake could shake him.
A poke or a pinch wouldn't budge him an inch,
'cause only his rooster could wake him.

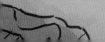

Then early one morning
(without any warning),
Rooster delivered a speech.
"I've saved up my money
to go someplace sunny.
I'm taking a trip to the beach!

I have it all planned.
I'll play in the sand.
My feathers will blow in the breeze.
I'll run in the sun
and have buckets of fun.
I'll sleep just as late as I please!"

"We don't want you to go!
If you do, who will crow?"
The animals cried, "This is bleak!"

"You'll each take a turn
'til the day I return.
I'll only be gone for a week."

"I'm sure I can do it.
There can't be much to it,"
said Pig, as he wallowed in mud.

He snorted with zeal,
Cock-a-doodle-**SQUEAL**!

His oink was an absolute dud!

Tuesday
Sheep

"I know that I'm quiet,
but I'd like to try it.
Here goes," said a shy little sheep.

Her cock-a-doodle baaaaaaa
didn't travel too faaa.
In fact, she made barely a peep!

"I'll teach you all how.
I'm a talented cow.
Step back and learn
from the master!"

A – one and a – two and a –
Cock-a-doodle-**MOoOOOO**!
Boy, what an udder disaster!

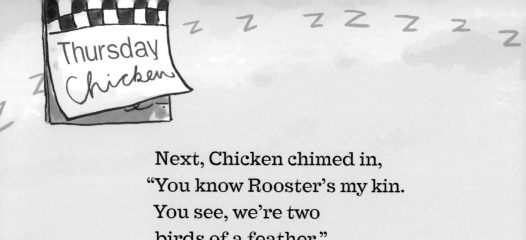

Next, Chicken chimed in,
"You know Rooster's my kin.
You see, we're two
birds of a feather."

Her **Cock-a-doodle-cluck** didn't have any pluck.

She blamed her weak voice on the weather!

Friday
Mule

Mule took on the task,
though he had to be asked.
As a matter of fact,
it took nudging.

He opened his jaw,

Cock-a-doodle-HEE-HAWWW!

His bray was a flop – but who's judging?

"I'll show you," said Goat,
after clearing his throat.
"I'm not just a kid anymore."

His **Cock-a-doodle-bleeeat** just couldn't compete with Farmer McPeeper's loud snore.

Sunday
Owl

"Don't throw in the towel,"
encouraged old Owl.
"I know I can do the job right."

Her Cock-a-doodle-whoooooooooooo
just didn't ring true.
(It's a fact - owls hoot
better at night.)

"Thank goodness you're back!
No time to unpack!
You've got to wake
Farmer McPeeper!

We each tried to crow
and by now we all know –
McPeeper's a very deep sleeper!"

Rooster coughed and he sputtered.
He wheezed and he muttered,

"There's something
I think you should know.
The damp ocean breeze
made me sniffle and sneeze.
My voice is so weak, I can't crow!"

"It's hopeless," said Goat.
"If he's got a sore throat,
    his crow will be too soft to hear.
Since Rooster can't do it
and each of us blew it,
    he'll probably sleep for a year!"

"I've got it," said Cow.
"We can wake him. Here's how:
we'll call from the
phone in the shed.
Rooster's crow will be near him,
so Farmer will hear him.
Let's hope there's a
phone by the bed."

Rooster pecked on the keys
with incredible ease.
They gathered around as it rang.

"You've reached the McPeepers,
please wait for the beeper."

He took a deep breath,
then he sang:

His crow finally worked!
Farmer woke with a jerk.

"My joints are so stiff that they creak.
My whiskers are stubbly,
my stomach's all grumbly.
It feels like I've slept for a week!"

He joined them outside
and pulled Rooster aside.

"Your crow had a bit of a screech.
I see that you're sick,
and I've got just the trick."

"What you need is . . .
a week at the beach!"